# Swords of Gregara - Jenala

CYNTHIA WOOLF

# DEDICATION

For Jim.  Without you I couldn't write.  I couldn't follow
my dream.  I love you.

# CONTENTS

# ACKNOWLEDGMENTS

To my critique partners, Michele Callahan, CJ Snyder, Karen Docter, Jennifer Zane and Kally Jo Surbeck, thank you.  Without your help and continued support I couldn't do what I do.

# CHAPTER 1

Swords clashed. Jenala Delasa fought savagely for her life against the man who would dare try to get her kalcion mine. And claim her. The bastard Zlaten Vandalar. The man she believed murdered her father six months ago. He attacked her with the intention of kidnapping and raping her, giving her no choice but to be claimed under the law. She'd fall on her own sword before she'd allow him to claim her. No, he attacked her in the narrow alleyway with every intention of kidnapping and raping her.

A passerby, having heard the gray metal swords clanging off of each other, sparks flying, and her shouts of rage, rushed to watch the spectacle. Jenala dared him a quick glance when he yelled and ran toward them. Momentarily startled, she missed her jab. Zlaten sidestepped, turned and flayed open her back from the left shoulder to the bottom of her ribcage on the right side. Jenala fell to the ground. Zlaten looked up at the stranger approaching and visibly paled. He sneered at her as he ran a finger through her blood that dripped from the tip of his sword. "You're not fit now. I'll come when you're healed then you'll be mine." He looked up at the stranger getting closer, turned and ran.

The stranger came to her, her sword still tightly gripped in her right hand. She'd dropped to her knees, never releasing her sword. The metallic taste of blood filled her mouth from where she'd bitten her tongue. She looked up with pain bleary eyes, expecting to see reproach or perhaps opportunity. If this man decided to claim her as Zlaten had, she could not fight him off. Instead she saw compassion. He removed his shirt and took great care to wrap her back to staunch the flow of blood. Jenala hissed at the contact, white flashing light blurred her vision. She knew he tried his best to cause her as little pain as possible, but it didn't matter, Jenala didn't know if she could handle the searing pain another moment. He picked her up and carried her toward town. The only person who could help was the town nupenian, who cared for animals. The quack they had for a doctor would surely kill her and she wasn't taking the chance. Brenton could sew her up as well as the doctor could.

"Take me to the nupenian," she said, her voice little more than a croak.

There hadn't been a decent doctor in Rucem, since she was born twenty-seven years ago. Dr. Nort had retired after delivering every baby, treating every illness and wound in the entire province for the previous forty years. Rucem was the capital and the largest outpost in the province. It was a months hard travel to get to the nearest large town with a doctor. The distance was so far, she'd only done it once with her father.

She must have lost consciousness, the

next thing she knew, she was looking up at a handsome man with a black eye patch and one gorgeous moss green eye.  The pain was gone.  Brenton must have provided her a pain blocker, thank Krios!  The man left instructions that she was to be taken to Wardsons Bedstay when the damage was fully sealed, though how he knew her accommodations she had no idea.  After the stranger left, Jenala wet her lips and finally asked.  "Well?  How does it look?"  She wiped at her mouth, afraid she'd drooled and it would be bloody on her face.

"It was a critical wound and will take time to heal.  You could have been killed.  You're lucky you were just laid open and it didn't get your kidney or some other necessary organ," said Brenton, the town nupenian.  He had been her father's best friend. Now he was Jenala's confident. Her father had been murdered six months ago and they both mourned the loss. What made the pain of his death even worse was the knowledge that his killer wanted her. Wanted to claim her. He'd even tried earlier and promised to return. Zlaten killed her father and wanted her. She couldn't prove his evil ways. She was being healed by a hand held med tech, from a wound he inflicted but unless the stranger came back it was a matter of Zlaten's word against hers. Hopefully, there would be enough to prove his guilt before he came back. To finish what he started and kill her.

"I'm going to give you something for the pain. I can't give you much because it's for tankipas and I don't know how well it's going to work"

"Thanks. If I could handle it, I'd go without anything but even I am not that masochistic."

"What in the world were you doing in that alley? Looking for Zlaten? Hoping to find him and goad him into fighting you? Jenala, what were you thinking?"

"I wasn't looking for him. He was stalking me. Brenton, he didn't attack me right away, though. He showed me some papers. It looked like Dad had signed them. They said that if Dad didn't pay back some loan, that Zlaten would be able to have me, unless I was already married. Do you know of this loan?"

Brenton hesitated, "He never intended for that clause to come to pass. He always expected to pay off the loan long before now."

"He would have claimed me had I let him, because he believes he has the right. He doesn't. I don't care what those papers may say, I will never be claimed or marry the man who murdered my father!"

"You're father would not have wanted you to. It was the only way he could get the money to start the mine. It was twenty years ago. He thought he would have plenty of time to pay it all back."

"Zlaten got too close, I didn't have Lottie to protect me so he thought he could get away with raping me to 'seal the bargain', he said. Thanks to that stranger he was wrong."

"Thank Krios for that. You must be more careful. And...you will have to marry someone else if you are to avoid having to marry him. If he takes those papers to the law, they likely will be upheld.  The only way out is if you marry before he claimed you.  Your father wanted you to be able to follow your heart.  He wanted you to marry for love.  Now you'll have to hurry and marry someone to avoid Zlaten."

"Don't lecture me, Brenton.  I'm thinking and hurting and wishing my father had told me of this long ago. Hell, would you rather that I'd just given over to Zlaten? Let him rape me in the alley?"

"No, of course not.  Your father would have flayed me as open as you are if I thought that for a minute."

"He's bold, bolder than he's ever been. Why didn't he show me the papers long ago?  Never mind.  He knows that I know he killed my father.  It was too soon after the attack.  But he's bold now.  Like he doesn't care who knows he killed Dad. He wants the mine and if he can't marry me, he'll kill me. That's the only other way.

"I don't know if I'll survive another attack. And he will return. I can't do this alone." She winced at the reseaming of the flesh on her back. "I need help. Do you know of anyone worthy? Worthy enough to marry? Oww." She looked over her shoulder and watched as he waived a hand held device over her wound.

"Sorry. Quit moving. Let the med unit do the work. How do you expect me to do this if you talk with your hands like you usually do? Plain old words will suffice, if you want me to finish this healing job. This machine wasn't made for use on humans so you will have a horrible scar."

"I don't care about the scar. No one but

me will ever see it.  I think your pain killer
is wearing off."  She was cranky and in pain.
And afraid.  Zlaten would have to kill her
because that was the only way he was
getting anything that belonged to her.  The
Delasa Mine was hers.  Her father left it to
her along with his considerable knowledge
of sword play.  It was the only thing that had
saved her this time.

"Brenton.  Who was the man who
brought me in here?  Zlaten ran from him
like he'd seen a ghost."  She tried not to
flinch as the wand he used did its work.  It
would seal the wound completely though
unlike a full size med tech, the interior
injury would take longer.  She would have a
couple of days of pain then she'd be better.
She'd still have to change the bandages once
per day.  They were there to provide support

for the new scar as much as anything else.

It was not going to be pretty when he was done and certainly not after it healed. This seam would close the wound, no more no less. She didn't really care. As long as she could work when she got back home.

"His name is Santro. He's been asking around about Zlaten. I think there is bad blood between them. Did you see the man's face?"

"Yes. He has a pleasant face."

"Pleasant face? Girl, the pain meds must be working or I haven't given you enough. I can only believe that you didn't really see him. He has a curved scar on his face from his right eye down to his chin. And considering the way he spat out Zlaten's name, I would guess he got the scar from that thieving, piece of zogamac dung."

Jenala laughed and regretted it immediately when Brenton skidded the wand across her skin.

"Hold still, would you?  I'm almost done.  Get that red hair of yours up and out of the way.  You've got a new seam across your back more than twelve inches long and I don't need your hair in it.  I've done the best I can with this portable med tech unit. What would help you most now, is rest, but I know you and know you won't rest as you need to, if at all.  I'm also going to give you an antibiotic shot.  We'll do our best to keep the wound from becoming infected."

"Now Brenton.  I'll do the best I can. You know that.  I'll stay at Wardson's Bedstay for one, maybe two days, and then I have to leave so I can get through the pass before the first snow of the season closes it again. All will be well when I reach my valley."

"If you survive. Done." He wrapped bandages around her ribcage from her arm pits to her belly button. "Here are some additional pills for pain. They're new, so remain at Wardson's until you're aware of your body's reactions before you get on that beast you call a pet."

"Lottie is a sweetheart and you know it." Jenala thought she might take one of the pills tonight and see how she felt, but there was no way she'd be in a stupor for two days on pain meds. Ashara! Just the thought of being that vulnerable left a bad taste in her mouth. Besides, there was only a twinge now where the skin was knitted together.

Brenton laughed. "She's a snarlot and

doesn't let anyone near her but you. She's the only reason you don't have more visitors in that valley of yours. Ashara! I might even visit if not for her."

"You would not and you know it. Galinda would never let you come alone. For a five year old, your daughter's very bossy. But you're right. Lottie's saved my hide numerous times. There's no doubt about that."

"With that beak, she can take on a zogamac and win. I still can't believe your father brought her back from Delaz for you. Do you remember how small she was when you got her?"

"Yes," she laughed and got a sharp pain in her back for the effort. "She was tiny, less than a foot tall. Runt of the litter. You know I measured her the other day and she's nearly eleven feet tall now! Not the runt of anything."

"Good grief. You'd need a ladder to get on if you hadn't taught her to bend her leg and let you crawl up."

She smiled. "I had to teach her so I could get the saddle on her. I made it you know, so I could ride and carry supplies at the same time. It's actually a good thing that she's so big, I don't need any pack tankipas that way." Brenton gave her the top to one of his uniforms to put on, her bloody shirt in tatters. "Thank you Brenton. May I pay you at a later time? I spent all my beras on supplies and the bedstay. I hadn't expected to be attacked in an alley by that bastard Zlaten. I won't make that mistake again.

"Sarina Wardson will offer extra days.

She knows my beras are good, as do you.
I'll have more kalcion from the mine.
Hopefully a lot more, but enough to pay
you. I promise."

"You know I'm not worried about it.
How's it going at the mine? You obviously
haven't hit the big vein yet."

"I know I'm so close. I'll find a little
vein and take a half bag out of it and it's
gone. So far it's only been enough to pay
my bills. But I know there's a mother lode
in there. Dad was sure of it and so am I."

"You're not the only one who thinks
there's a rich vein in that mine of yours. The
Delasa kalcion mine is legend. You know
that. There are hundreds of stories about it
and the kalcion hidden there. So, your
beautiful self isn't the only thing that Zlaten
wants from you."

"I know. The mine is what brought him here in the first place. I'm just the easy way to get it. At least he thought so until tonight. Now he knows he'll have to kill me just as he did my father."

"He won't give you a second chance, you know. Given the way he killed your father, you need to be on guard or he'll stab you in the back as well."

"I'm all too aware of that. Thanks for healing me. I do appreciate it, even if I whine a bit." She kissed his cheek and made her way to the Bedstay, conscious of the revived skin and tissue pulling at her back.

*****

Santro heard the clash of metal on metal coming from the alley to his left. He walked over intending to watch the outcome of what was likely young men trying their mettle against each other.

What he saw momentarily left him frozen. There in from of him was Zlaten Vandalar fighting with a red haired woman. The woman appeared to be holding her own against the evil man she fought. Coming to his senses Santro yelled at Zlaten. "Stop."

The woman glanced at him and Zlaten moved in. She missed her jab, Zlaten swiveled, slashing her along her back. Then he looked up at Santro, paled, said something to the woman, turned and ran out the other end of the alley.

Santro went to the woman, on her knees now, sword still clasped tight in her hand. She looked up at him, fear clearly in her eyes. He took off his shirt to staunch the blood that flowed freely down her back. Her fear was replaced by relief. He felt it radiate from her.

He was unable to tell how serious the wound was, only that a lot of blood covered her now. He wrapped her in his shirt as gently as he could. Then picked her up in his arms and started out of the alley. As soon as he picked her up he felt an electricity up his arms and down to his groin. Never had he felt that with any woman. And to feel it now. Well it was damn inconvenient.

"Take....me...to...the...nupenian. Not the doctor, the nupenian." She said it, gasping in between words.

She was light in his arms. He ran with her to the nupenian whose office he'd passed not long ago. It was lucky they were close, though why she'd want to go to the animal doctor, he didn't know. But he would take her.  She was in too much pain for him to go looking for the regular doctor anyway.

He burst through the door of the nupenian, "I have an injured woman here. She insisted that I bring her to you."

The nupenian looked up.  "Jenala! Come, put her on my examination table face down."

As soon as he put her on the table, she released her sword and it clattered to the floor.

Santro watched him remove his bloody shirt and then the girls, cutting it away from the angry wound.  It looked worse from here now that the shirt wasn't covering it.  "Will she be all right?"

"I don't know yet.  What happened?"

"She was fighting with Zlaten Vandalar

in an alley near here. I'm afraid I distracted her from her fight and Zlaten wounded her before he ran away like the coward he is."

"I'm Brenton and he's not just a coward, he's a murderer as well. Killed her father six months ago, though she can't prove it. Not yet any way. Who are you?" He talked while he worked cleaning the wound. Now that Santro could see it, he couldn't believe that she still held her sword until he'd brought her in here. The wound was a long, angry slash from her left shoulder to her waist on the right. It had to be more than twelve inches long.

"My name is Santro Baltin."

"You'll find a shirt in the cupboard above the sink. Thank you for bringing her to me."

"She would go nowhere else. The only

thing she said to me was to bring her here."

"Considering her wound I'm surprised she was still conscious enough to tell you. She's a very strong woman."

"I can see that." Amazing was more like it. He'd never seen any woman fight like that. She'd obviously been trained from an early age to fight. Why would anyone take the time to train a woman. Extraordinary.

"Will you see that she is taken to the Bedstay in town after she is healed. You can heal her can't you?"

"The instruments I have are not for people. They are for animals with much thicker skin than Jenala. I'll do the best I can but I'm going to have to set it low. It will seal the wound against further blood loss, but she will still need to heal on the inside."

Santro watched Brenton move the med tech wand slowly over the wound. Back and forth until the wound sealed. He would do a small section at a time, sealing and moving on. It would take it quite a while to seal the whole wound.

"I must leave."

Brenton pulled the wand away from Jenala's wound, put it in his left hand and held out his right. "I can't thank you enough for coming to her aid. She is like a daughter to me. Anything you need that I can do for you, let me know."

"There is something. I need to know where Zlaten Vandalar is staying or camping. Would you know?"

"You'll be better off talking to Jenala when she is better. Vandalar is squatting in her valley."

Santro looked down at the girl on the table. He would have her help with or without her knowledge.

*****

Jenala stopped in the entry and asked Sarina to send a tray to her room. Right now all she wanted was another one of those pills Brenton gave her and then her bed. She knew there was no way in Ashara that she'd be able to be in the company of other people and be a decent guest for dinner.

Her back throbbed. The sooner she got additional rest to restore the remaining wounded tissue, the better off she'd be.

As she headed to the stairs she saw Santro enter the lobby. Now that her mind wasn't muddled with pain, she recognized how attractive a man he was. A flash of need traveled from her breasts to her core and took her by surprise. She remembered the play of his muscles as he carried her. Even through her pain she felt a strong attraction to him.

He may have only one eye, but the moss green with golden flecks was striking. Especially with the shock of dark, almost black hair with copper streaks at the temples. He was tall, lean and strong. She remembered him running with her in his arms. She could see now that his arms were incredibly muscular. He was well used to using the sword at this side. She remembered those strong arms cradling her so gently. The shirt and pants he wore fit him incredibly well. Highlighting his long legs, flat abdomen and wide shoulders.

She walked over to him. She saw a flash of lust at her approach, yet when she looked up at him again, it was gone. "Thank you. You probably saved my life today." She noticed his clean scent, like he was fresh from a bath though his hair wasn't wet so she could only surmise that he smelled this wonderful all the time.

"You're welcome." His gaze raked her body, "Why did he attack you? Do you know him?"

"His name is Zlaten Vandalar. He wants my mine, among other things. Why are you looking for him?"

Santro's eye narrowed and his mouth turned down. Anger radiated from him. "Who said I was?"

"It was rather obvious he's afraid of you. You appeared and he fled. It wasn't just that you came upon him fighting a woman, and losing I might add. No, there was definite fear in his eyes."

"He killed my brother."

"Ah," she nodded. "I'm sorry for your loss. It would appear we have this in common. I believe he murdered my father. I'm Jenala Delasa."

He took her extended hand and shook it. "Santro Baltin. Would you care to dine with me this evening, Jenala?"

"I'd love to, but I'm afraid my wound is getting the best of me and I must go take my medication."

He nodded, "I understand."

"Perhaps we can make it breakfast tomorrow instead?"

Smiling, he said, "I'd like that if you are well enough. I'll meet you here at seven."

"Very good."

Santro bowed to her. "Until then."

In her room Jenala carefully unwrapped her bandages. She wanted to see the damage that Zlaten had wrought on her body. The reflection in the mirror showed an angry, uneven line of healing flesh more than a foot long across her back. Brenton was right; it was not going to be pretty. Ashara, it wasn't pretty now, but it was improving by the minute thanks to the med tech wand Brenton used.

She got the pill bottle from what was left of her coat. Something else she'd have to do tomorrow. Repair the slash in her coat. Hopefully Sarina had needle and thread because she hadn't brought hers with her. It may be fall but snow was still likely. She still wouldn't be able to go through the mountains with no coat, even riding Lottie.

Jenala had a restless, painful night. The

pills Brenton gave her took the edge off the discomfort of her flesh remorphing but not entirely. She got very little sleep. Every time she turned on to her back she awoke. She'd get up take another pill and pace the small room. From the window across the room to the door. In front of the bed back and forth. She tried sitting at the small desk and reading but she couldn't concentrate. All she could think of was Santro. How he'd taken care of her. Without asking he'd carried her and made her feel safe. Really safe for the first time since her father died.

Finally she rolled to her stomach, took another pain pill and washed it down with Darinda brandy. By the time the sun rose she was dressed.

She made her way downstairs to the meal room for a cup of hot aeta before meeting Santro. He must have had the same trouble sleeping she'd had because he was already sitting at a table when she entered the dining room.

"You seem to be an early riser. Unfortunately, my back has turned me into one as well. Would you mind eating a little earlier?"

"Of course not. I kept hoping you would come down sooner."

She smiled. "That's sweet of you. Why would you hope that? I would have thought you'd had enough of me. I've been nothing but trouble to you since you first laid eyes on me. And I believe I owe you a shirt."

Santro laughed, a dimple appeared where his scar ended. "A beautiful woman is never trouble but you do indeed owe me a shirt." Then he gestured to the vacant chair across from him. "Please sit."

He stood and pulled out the chair for her. She sat gingerly, ever cautious of her back.

"I see your back is bothering you this morning. The nupenian, Brenton, told me that you would still have to heal on the inside."

"Yes, it's healing well on the outside but inside it's still quite injured. He has me wrapped in bandages to aid the process. His were rather tight. I unwrapped myself last night, which was a mistake, as I had a very difficult time trying to rewrap them myself. I have to go back to Brenton and have him wrap me back up. Then I'll have to come back here and take another pain pill. I did find that Darinda brandy makes them go down so much easier." She wiggled and straightened her back trying to relieve the pain.

"He seemed like a competent man and you were quite relieved when we reached his office. So much so that you passed out."

She laughed at that. "I was in a little bit of pain, if you remember. Seriously, he's a good friend and more competent than any doctor we've had since…I don't remember the last time we had a good doctor. Probably when I was born."

The waitress came to take their order. Santro ordered eggs with tequati, toast and coffee. "I acquired a taste for the Earth beverage when I was being fostered by Sunev."

"I've tried it, I still prefer my aeta." She placed her order for the same plus fried sunda root and aeta.

"Where did you learn the way of the sword?" asked Santro. "There aren't a lot of women in my tribe that use it."

"There aren't a lot of women anywhere that use the sword. My father taught me."

"Of course," he said putting two and two together. "Your father was Oliria Delasa, the master swordsman. I knew your father. He was a good friend to the man that fostered me."

Their breakfast arrived and Jenala dug in with gusto. She swallowed "Ah, I needed some food. All those pain pills and no food was making me nauseous. I couldn't eat last night, I was hurting too bad. Now I'm ravenous."

"By all means, please eat."

She took another bite before she spoke again. "I don't remember my father mentioning you."

"He wouldn't have. I was just a boy. But he would have probably talked of my teacher, Sunev, who's now my good friend."

"Yes, Sunev is a name I know. I met him once at the annual kalcion market in Sepiwa. A large man with clear green eyes. Eyes the color of a jewel. Yours on the other hand, are the color of early spring moss with flecks of gold. Very nice."

He blushed. Jenala had made the big man blush. "Thank you. It is kind that you noticed my eye."

"Noticed it?" She laughed. "It's rather hard not to notice it. We should get this out right away because I sense it troubles you. I do not find your scar unattractive. It is simply a part of the person I know as Santro. Scars are the mark of a warrior. I have my own scars, including the new one Zlaten gave me yesterday. It is a flesh wound. A *long, deep* flesh wound, but a flesh wound nonetheless. Your wound was much more serious. Did Zlaten give you that one?"

"Yes. He challenged me for Valmud of the Otulas. He cheated. Threw something into my face that made it burn. I couldn't see to block all of his blows and lost my eye. I couldn't prove his treachery at the time. After I was wounded, he challenged my younger brother and killed him. That time the council saw Zlaten throw the acid powder into Kreston's face. He was arrested and the council agreed to let me seek 'justice'. He fled before sentencing."

"So now you're hunting him, correct?"

"Yes."

There was something about this man.

He was inherently honorable and trustworthy. She felt it deep in her bones and she knew it from his story of Zlaten's treachery. She made a quick decision and didn't mince words, "I have a proposition I would like to run by you. I need help with Zlaten and my mine. Zlaten has disappeared for the moment, as you're well aware, but I know he will be lying in wait for me somewhere along the way unless I leave before he does. He wants to claim me and my mine. I can't let either one of those things happen."

She saw Santro's jaw clench.

"I propose you come with me for the winter, assuming you have no other obligations that would prevent it.

"You could help me work my mine. I will give you fifty percent of the ore and you can help me keep watch for Zlaten. He will be encamped in my valley, where he's been for the last two weeks. The only thing that has kept him from killing me is Lottie. He'll be trying to get me and my mine. I guarantee it. If you stay here, you won't get the opportunity to confront him. I can give him to you. He will be harassing me, perhaps even try to kill me. At the very least he will rape me and instantly claim me for life." Now it was her turn to clench her jaw.

"Your home is large enough to accommodate me?"

"Yes. I've never had guests, but there are two bedrooms. You would have my old room. I have moved into my father's room."

"I will take you up on your offer. At least for the winter."

"Good." She'd finished her breakfast, every last morsel and was sipping her aeta. She held her cup with two hands and looked down into it. "You also need to come meet someone after we eat."

"Who is that?" Santro said between mouthfuls.

"Lottie…my…uh…snarlot."

"Snarlot?" He choked on his coffee. "You have a snarlot?"

"Yes, she can easily carry two and makes incredible time through the mountains," Jenala said quickly.

"You *ride* a snarlot. They can tear a zogamac limb from limb with that beak of theirs. They are ten feet of snarling, chirping beast. Do you have any idea how dangerous that is or how dangerous a snarlot is? "

"Of course, I do. I'm not an idiot. But

39

Lottie is a big softy where I'm concerned. She's saved my hide from Zlaten more than once.   We'll have to see how she feels about you."

"Great," groaned Santro.

"It'll be fine.  You'll see.  You'll need supplies.  I'm afraid I didn't lay in enough for two.  I can't pay you before the ore is dug and we sell the kalcion at the annual market."

"No problem.  I'll get my supplies.  I have enough beras from my former work as a malitin hunter.  Though this time it is personal."

"My mine is a one man operation up until now.  Of course when Father was alive we both worked the mine."

"Woman."

"What?"

"A one woman operation. Even I, with one eye, can see that you, with your fiery hair and sapphire blue eyes, are not a man." His one eyed gaze raked over her body. Jenala felt her nipples tighten at the heat she saw there.

Jenala laughed, covering her nervousness at her body's response to just a glance from Santro. "I'm glad to see you have a sense of humor. It will make the time pass much more quickly." Suddenly she was serious. "You intend to kill him, do you not? Because if you don't, I will." She wasn't boasting or threatening. She meant it. She would kill him, not for what he did to her, that was secondary. No, she would kill him for murdering her father.

"I will kill him or die trying. I can't sleep if I let him go unpunished."

"Agreed.  You will get your chance, I promise you."

## CHAPTER 2

The next morning, Santro met Lottie.

She was eleven feet of snarling, chirping beast. Perhaps the biggest snarlot he'd ever seen and certainly the only one he'd seen this close up.

Dark brown fur covered her from her pointy, tiny eared, beaked head to her hoofed feet. She had a whip of a tail covered with hair interspersed with quills. Get too close and she'd shoot one at you, closer still and she could snap her tail and take your hand off without letting loose a single quill.

If her tail wasn't dangerous enough, her beak was filled with razor sharp teeth that could rip your arm off with one bite. To top this all off, the damn thing purred.

Santro stood next to Jenala and stared. There were few things that put the fear of the divine into him. Lottie was one of them. Lottie didn't like him. He knew it. Could feel the hostility.

"Come on, I'll introduce you," Jenala said as she walked up to the beast.

"I think I'll stay right here. I can meet her from a distance."

"Don't be silly. You have to ride her, in order to do that you need to meet her. Just follow my lead." Jenala when up to Lottie and hugged her. "Lottie my sweet girl, this is Santro." She motioned for Santro to step forward and as he did she took his hand. Electricity shot up his arm. Suddenly his fear of the snarlot was nothing. He'd ride the snarlot or a zogamac or any other wild beast just to be near to her. He'd never felt this kind of immediate all consuming attraction for anyone before. It took him by surprise and left him breathless for a moment.

"He's going to be with us for a while, so I want you to be nice." Jenala said to the snarlot, petting her neck. Lottie's purr was so loud it almost resonated through him.

He approached Lottie slowly. She bent down and first, smelled him. He held his breath and his heart thundered in his chest. Then she looked him in the eye. He held completely still, afraid that if he moved she'd think it was aggression and attack. She closed her eyes and nudged him with her head, asking for a scratch. Santro obliged. He let out his breath. Much to his relief, he'd passed the test.

Jenala gave him a brilliant smile. "See, I told you it would be okay. Lottie doesn't let anyone near her. As a matter of fact, you're the first."

"I'm honored." And thankful he amended to himself. He wasn't sure what he'd done if Lottie hadn't accepted him.

"You should be. If she hadn't liked you we'd have to find another mode of transport for you and then wouldn't make it through the pass before the first snow of the season. As it is we will be in the valley a good week before Zlaten and his thugs."

"Good. We'll need the time to prepare."

"What do you have in mind?"

Santro had given this a bit of thought last night between trying to sleep and picturing the beautiful woman he'd just partnered with gloriously naked. The real reason he was doing this was the woman. She was magnificent. Fighting toe to toe with Zlaten and holding her own, even winning. If he hadn't shouted at Zlaten and distracted her, she would have won. He recognized her skill and was impressed. Her wound was his fault. He should have just charged forward and engaged Zlaten.

"We need to protect the perimeter and set up an alarm system in not only the house but the mine as well. The warning systems need to be set so we have enough time to get back to the house from the mine."

"That won't be a problem."

"You already have alarms set up?"

"No. That's a good idea though. I was talking about getting from the mine to the house. That won't be a problem. The entrance to the mine is in the house."

"Clever. No one can find it and pilfer your ore that way."

"True. Not that there's much to pilfer.

***** 

The trip to the valley was long and arduous, even on Lottie it took ten hours. It would take Zlaten on his tankipa three days to cover the same amount of ground. They would arrive way before Zlaten.

Jenala thought they'd miss the first snow but it was early and caught them as they reached the top of pass. They took the saddle off of Lottie and headed inside of the shelter shack to wait for the storm to pass.

Lottie had thick fur that helped keep her warm and there was a lean-to that kept the bulk of the wind and snow off of her. But Jenala and Santro had to find another way to keep warm.

The attack came just as they entered the shack. Three men waited for them. Santro took on two of them and Jenala one. The attack happened so fast they didn't have time to do anything but unsheathe their swords and block the first blows. The sound of metal ringing on metal was deafening. Jenala felt herself weakening. She had to get outside, Lottie would help her. She backed up parrying each of the blows as they came. Finally she was at the door. She reached around and pulled open the door, backing out of it as she continued to block the blows.

"Lottie," she yelled.

She didn't have to wait; the noise had brought Lottie to the shack. She waited outside howling with the wind. As soon as Jenala saw her she slashed back at her opponent, forcing him back long enough for her to turn and run behind Lottie.

The snarlot charged forward, her beak closing on the man's head. She lifted him and shook her head. Even over the howling of the storm, Jenala heard his neck break, then with a final shake, his body separated from his head falling to the blood covered ground.

Jenala ran back to the shack. She had to help Santro. Pulling open the door she ran inside only to see Santro pull his sword from the gut of one of the assailants. The second one had fallen in a corner of the room and though not dead his arm was severed and he was screaming, holding his hand over the wound. He was bleeding out, quickly. He would be dead within minutes.

Santro turned quickly toward her, sword up, ready for the next opponent. When he saw her, he wiped his sword on his opponents shirt and then sheathed it, before walking to her and taking her in his arms. She fell into them, wrapped her arms around his neck and held on for dear life.

"Lottie saved me. I couldn't fight. My back wound, I'm too weak."

"It's all right. Everything's all right."

They stood there for a few minutes, just holding each other, both breathing hard, neither saying a word.

Santro was the first one to pull back. "We have to get these bodies out of here.

The storm is not going to let up for who knows how long and I refuse to share our lodgings with this vermin."

The man in the corner was no longer making any noise. He leaned against the wall, his eyes still open, not moving. He was dead.

Santro grabbed the man's shoulders, Jenala his feet and they dragged him out into the storm, throwing his body next to the shack. They did the same with the other man. Lottie had taken care of the third man, hauling his body into the surrounding forest.

They went back inside the shack. It was covered in blood, but it was out of the storm. It had some wood for the stove, a small table with two chairs and many games on a shelf. There was also a bed. A small bed with barely room enough for two people, but

Jenala knew that they would have to use it together to keep warm. The firewood was not enough to last the night and would have to be used sparingly.

Santro caught her staring at the bed. "I promise I won't bite," he said with a smile.

She blushed. "Of course, you don't. I'm just…just…," she stammered.

He came forward and lifted her chin with his knuckle until she looked at him. "Look at it this way, you've already been in my arms, this will be no different. I'll hold you so we can both stay warm. On my honor, I will not take advantage of you."

She looked up into his face and saw the truth. He would keep her safe.

He changed the subject. "Tell me about Zlaten. Why do you think he murdered your father? Don't misunderstand, I believe you.

I want to know the why and the how."

"Father was home alone. I'd gone to town on Lottie to get more lumber and other supplies. He'd hit a particularly large crack of kalcion. Not the major vein by any means, but larger than any we'd found in a quite awhile. It yielded enough for us to stock up on things we needed. We hadn't been able to do that for a long time.

"Zlaten Vandalar was at the ore exchange when I cashed it in. I saw him in there and only one tankipa was outside the exchange, so it had to be his. It is a black and white paint. Very unusual for this area.

"When I got home I found my father dead in Lottie's barn and that same paint colored tankipa racing out of the valley. There was no one else around. As you'll see, the view from the front of the dome covers the entire valley."

"Did you know Zlaten?"

"No. I'd never met him."

"How did he find you?"

Rubbing the cold from her arms she answered him. "He asked at the exchange for my father. They gave him directions. My father was a well known sword master. It was not unusual for people to seek him out for instruction. It was how he supported us most of the time."

"But you don't think that Zlaten came for lessons?" he asked while stoking the fire. He wanted to pull her into his arms, give his warmth to her and kiss her senseless but he couldn't, Not yet. He would earn her trust before he learned her body and tasted her essence. Before he made her his.

"No. He saw me exchange my ore for

beras and thought he could threaten my father into selling the mine for nothing. When Father would not sell the Delasa mine Zlaten killed him." Tears flowed freely down her face. "I found Father with his own sword in his back." She pounded the table with her fist. "He killed him and I can't prove it. He attacked me and still roams free because there is no law to apprehend him."

Santro took her in his arms, his hatred for Zlaten Vandalar grew as did his feelings for Jenala. "I'm sorry for your loss. It's never easy losing a parent, no matter the circumstances of their death."

She sniffled. "Being an only child, I cannot imagine losing a sibling. It must be difficult. Were you close to your brother?"

"Kreston was my best friend. Zlaten will pay for his murder."

A short while later, Jenala could barely keep her eyes open. She got into bed and moved over to the wall, as far as she could. Santro joined her, took her into his arms and held her close. She slept warm, safe from the world, all night.

They started down the mountain toward Jenala's home. About half way down, there was an overlook where you could see the entire valley. Santro whistled.

"Beautiful, isn't it?" said Jenala, proud of her home.

"Amazing. It's got to be one of the most beautiful places on the planet."

"I think so." And it was all hers. From the verdant green fields where she grew vegetables in the summer, to the high pastures and low meadows where Lottie ran free, to the river with large tequati ripe for catching. It was hers. There were wild emul in the forest. She killed and cured the meat for eating in winter when game was scarce.

What did Santro see? Did he only see the beauty or did he see the hard work involved in keeping the valley safe as well as beautiful?

"Tell me about this valley of yours. Start with the river. Where does it lead?"

"The river leaves the valley through a canyon with sheer cliff walls. It's full of killer rapids and is unnavigable because of them. As you can see the valley is surrounded on the other three sides by mountains. This pass is the only way into or out of the valley. The other two mountains are too steep and too rocky to have a pass through them." She let out a sigh. "You're probably wondering why I don't just hire someone to guard the pass. The reason is I have no money. Hence my arrangement with you. I'm desperate, Santro. I need your help."

He tightened his arms around her waist. "And you have it. Let's go see this house of yours."

The house sat on a bluff on the north side overlooking the valley. From the front door Jenala saw the river to the east flowing south. Light green meadow dotted with wildflowers covered the valley floor and the pass they'd just come through was on the west side. The mountain sides were dark green with forest followed by brown, rocky slopes up to the summits, all of which were covered with a light dusting of snow.

By this time he thought he'd gotten use

to Lottie's odd gait but when she took off down the mountainside headed for home it was all he could do to hold on to Jenala and not fall off the running beast. Jenala was used to this and laughed, the wind blowing through her flaming red hair. She looked like some ancient warrior princess leading her troops through the pass to their next battle.

When they reached the house, Jenala scrambled down, underneath Lottie and unsaddled her. When she'd finished she patted her and said, "There you go girl. That feels better doesn't it?" The snarlot headed for the river where she caught her supper. Lottie always provided for herself when at home. When they traveled, Jenala fed her raw emul meat that she froze just for that purpose. Occasionally, she would give her some as a treat when they were home.

Santro helped her take the supplies into the house. "This is much bigger than it appears from the outside."

"You noticed we came down stairs as soon as we entered. The entire house is built down into the bluff." She pointed to the ceiling. "The only part showing above ground is the glass dome. It allows the sunlight which in turn heats the house. All the rooms are open to it."

"I guess that means no sleeping late around here."

"Not if you leave the ceiling shade open." She smiled proud of her home, the home her father had built for them. "Each room has its own privacy shade. It keeps out the light *and* prying eyes. It also helps keep the room cool in summer. We won't have need of it this time of year, except for the light filtering."

She showed him to her old bedroom. "This is it. I hope you'll be comfortable. The entrance to the mine is in my bedroom, which was my father's and is on the opposite side of the house. He sometimes worked long into the night and thoughtfully," she smiled at the memory, "didn't want to subject his teenage daughter to the noise of late night drilling."

Jenala showed Santro the mine entrance at the back of her closet. It opened when a button, hidden on the floor, was depressed. The mine itself was well lit, down to the latest drill site. The floor was dirt and the walls were braced with wood planks.

Impressed, Santro asked, "How much of this have you completed since your father's death?"

"Only the last ten meters. Even with Lottie's help it's hard getting the wood braces to the house much less into the mine. You noticed that it's a straight shot from the front door through the house to Dad's room and into the mine. Now you know why. It's for the braces. We had to be able to bring in long pieces of wood to reinforce the sides and ceiling of the mine."

"Ten meters is a long way to dig and brace. I'm amazed you've been able to do that much. It would be difficult for a man alone much less a woman."

She cocked an eyebrow. "You must not know many strong women."

"You're right, I don't. The women of my tribe do not wield swords nor do they work in the mines."

"Don't you know any women that use swords? I can't be the only one out there."

"I personally know only one. Her name is Kitari Dolana. She is Sunev's daughter and only recently started her sword training. She is fanatical about it though. Remind me to tell you the full story during one of our long winter nights." He thought of a few other things he'd like for them to do on those long nights but talking would do. For a start. By the end of winter he meant for Jenala to be his. The attraction he felt intensified with each moment he spent with her. His heart raced and whenever he touched her, even in passing, she was burned more deeply into his consciousness.

"I will. She sounds fascinating. So what do the women of your tribe do?"

"They cook, clean, care for the children.

The men do all the mining and the fighting."

"The fighting must keep you busy. I'm surprised you have time for anything else."

Santro didn't miss the sarcasm. "I suppose to you our females seem oppressed. I assure you they are not. All careers are open to both sexes, it is a conscious choice by the women when they decide not to learn the sword or work in the mines. But enough of this talk. It's time to rest and eat some of the tasty tequati that I'm going to catch for our dinner. Why don't you prepare some tingo root to go with it? I'll return shortly."

\*\*\*\*\*

The previous day's journey from town and moving the lumber through the house and into the mine took more out of her than she'd admit. Jenala was exhausted and fell into bed. The next morning she could barely move and her back was on fire. She'd slept in a soft shirt of her father's for modesty. Normally she slept in the nude. The shirt was stuck to her back and she knew that she'd bled through it when she saw the spots on her sheets.

"Santro," she called. She was a little anxious, hoping that she hadn't ripped open the seam. She didn't want to have to sit through being stitched up by Santro without any anesthetic. It would hurt like hell. "Santro!"

"What is it?" he said from her doorway, rubbing his face and the sleep from his eyes.

"I think I opened the seam. I need your help after I remove this shirt. You'll need to tell me how much of the seam has opened. If it's small enough you can just put a liquid sealer on it and redo the bandage.

Otherwise you'll have to stitch me."

"Are you sure you want me to do this? Maybe we should go back to town."

"Don't be ridiculous. The trip to town takes hours and we need to start work on the alarms and setting them up." She opened the shirt front and ripped it off her back from where the blood had dried. She tried not to but couldn't stop a small scream of pain. She leaned forward, both hands on her dresser and rested.

Santro stood behind her, she watched him in the mirror. He winced when she ripped her shirt, then he noticed the mirror and his eyes got wide. She followed his eyes and saw he was staring at her breasts. She fell forward on to her elbows. His attention refocused to her back and he was all business.

"I need to clean your back before I can be certain what is open. There is dried blood and some fresh from you ripping off your shirt. It would probably be easiest on you if you could soak it off, but if it has come open flooding it with water may not be good for it."

Jenala straightened and held the shirt in front of her. She wasn't normally modest and had only worn the shirt in case of a leak. But it appeared her breasts were a distraction for Santro. "The medical supplies are in the bathroom."

Santro turned and went into Oliria's bath with Jenala on his heels. The bath was attached to the bedroom opposite the closet and mine entrance.

"The medical bag is in the cabinet under the sink. You should find everything you need in it."

"Come over here. Let's get it cleaned before we do anything else."'

Jenala walked over and turned her bared back to him. Santro turned on the water and got it warm before he soaked the cloth and pressed it to her back.

She sucked in her breath at the contact, but didn't step away. Though at that moment there was nothing more she wanted to do than move away from the gentle hands that washed her back. She was surprised such a fierce man could have such a gentle way about him. He was being exceedingly careful to hurt her as little as possible while he cleaned her wounds.

"Well, there is good news. It doesn't appear you've opened the seams very much. They mostly seeped and that is why your shirt stuck to you. I'm going to put some of this salve you have in here on them and then bind you tightly. It will not be very comfortable, but it will help to keep the seams from seeping again."

"Thank you. I appreciate your help. Let's just get it done so we can get started on the alarms."

Santro did his best to stay detached. He'd been thunderstruck when she'd ripped her shirt from her back and then again when he saw her breasts in the mirror. They were perfect. High, round, tipped pale pink, perfect for his tongue to twirl around. The long coil of bright red hair she'd thrown over her shoulder stood in stark contrast to her white skin. Unfortunately for him it also covered one of her beautiful breasts.

The agony she'd tried to suppress

showed in her dark blue eyes and forced him to focus his attention to her back. The long, angry wound was covered in dried blood. He soaked as much as possible from it.

"It's a good thing you at least have the liquid bandage. I don't know if either one of us would survive my efforts to stitch you up the old fashioned way."

"If we don't get Zlaten, I will have to invest in a healing wand. Probably should anyway. This is not the first injury I've had that needed one. It's just the worst."

He poured the liquid bandage on the part of the wound that had ripped open.

She hissed. It was not a painless solution. The liquid stung and smelled awful, but it did the job and closed the small tear in the seam.

He then covered it in the antibiotic salve

from the medical kit, put bandages on the wound then bound her chest tightly. It pained him to flatten her wonderful breasts with the tight bandage, but there was nothing else he could do. The wound on her back needed to heal and would only do so if it could be immobilized. He couldn't see her staying in bed for days while it did that, so the tight bandage around her ribcage would have to do.

"Face me and lift your arms out so I can wrap the bandage. If the bandage doesn't hold…" he left it hanging in the air, both of them knew what would happen if the bandages didn't hold. She would have to be stitched. Not a happy prospect for either one of them.

She turned to face him. Her breasts firm and full, bare to him. It required all his will power and concentration not to bend and take one taut nipple into his mouth and suck until she moaned in ecstasy.

"There, that should do it.  It needs to stay on tight for a couple of days and you will not be able to bathe during that time." He grinned at her, "I am preparing myself for you to start smelling like Lottie."

She laughed, as he'd hoped she would.

## CHAPTER 3

Zlaten and his men waited to enter the valley under the cover of darkness and then camped in the forest near the river. That beast snarlot she called a pet nearly trampled their camp during the first night but had moved on before finding them.

He watched the house from a distance. Watched Santro help the girl secure it, as if an alarm would keep him away. He didn't see them secure the mine, still didn't know where it was. He was sure that once he was done, Santro would leave, go back to his hunt, never knowing how close he was to his prey. But he was wrong. Zlaten watched for days and Santro didn't leave. He stayed with the girl. Appeared to be living with her. Had he given up the hunt or did he know that his quarry was in the valley. Had the girl told him about her father? Obviously, she had and now Santro waited for him.

*****

Jenala and Santro designed and set the alarm system. They knew Zlaten was camped in the valley. He may have come in during the night but the smoke from his campfire was easily spotted in the morning. Did he not realize they would be able to see it or did he not care? They waited for him to make a move, while they worked in the mine.

Jenala insisted Santro help her rig the mine to explode should they lose the battle if there was one. They figured that he would most likely try to ambush them when they were bringing in more timber, but wanted to be prepared for any contingency. She was determined that even if she lost her life, Zlaten was not going to take everything she and her father had worked for.

"My bandages should come off tonight. You'll need to see if the wound is healed enough for me to stop wearing the wrapping."

"Yes. Hopefully we'll be able to leave them off. It should have healed enough in the last two weeks that the scar won't need the support of the bandages any longer."

"Thank you for taking care of my back.

I couldn't have done it myself. I would have had to do nothing when I got home if you hadn't been here to bind me. I'd guess this was not your first time having to play doctor."

"Yes, well, the Valmud must be prepared for all things."

"You were Valmud of the Otulas? Should I be honored by your presence here?"

Santro laughed but there was no joy in the sound. "I was never Valmud. I lost the fight with Zlaten, when he threw a powder into my face. He was very subtle about it. It was laced with a substance that made my entire face feel like it was on fire. I dropped my guard and his sword took my eye. To this day I don't know what the substance was. His trickery went undetected and he won the right to challenge the Valmud, my father. My brother, being the next in line, challenged Zlaten to combat instead. Zlaten did the same thing to my brother, except Kreston was killed instead of just scarred. The council saw the deception this time but Zlaten fled before he could be tried for murder. He came here to escape me."

"I'm sorry about Kreston and I do understand. Zlaten thinks to start over with my mine but he is sadly mistaken. My father may have turned his back on him, but I won't make the same mistake. Zlaten has no honor. When he attacked me in the alley, he may have tried to get close enough to do something like that to me. But I kept him at sword length and managed to keep my guard up. At least until he slashed and ran…from you. Will you challenge him to a duel?"

"I will. I most certainly will not ambush him, which is what I believe he's waiting to do to us."

"He's afraid of you. He knows he can't best you in a fair fight. That's why he's waiting…watching. I wish he'd go ahead a make his move. The waiting is intolerable."

"You find my company so terrible, do you?" asked Santro with a smile.

"No, of course not. You know what I mean. Stop teasing me." She laughed with him before becoming serious. "It's been two weeks and he still just watches. He's made no moves. He and the five men he has with them act like they are on some vacation. Camping out in my valley, fishing my river and eating the emul in my forest. I'd stop them if I thought I could before they killed me."

"I know. It's like something is in the offing and we don't know what but he does. Is there any way off this bluff, without being seen? We could perhaps do some reconnaissance."

"The only way would be using the cover of darkness then go out the back, across to Lottie's barn and down the bluff through the forest on the other side of her barn. We could actually follow behind Lottie on her nightly rounds. They have to have gotten used to the noise she makes by now and won't notice our movements."

"We'll try it tonight, if the moon isn't too bright. Agreed?"

"Agreed," said Jenala.

*****

Mining was hard, back breaking work, when you were doing it all by hand. You drilled a bit, then shoveled the rocks, then drilled some more. Once the cart was full it was taken to the front of the mine and sifted, checking for kalcion nuggets or flakes.

They worked side by side all day, with very little to show for it. A couple of minor cracks yielded enough ore to buy a day or two supplies. The only other thing they had to show for their efforts were sore, tired bodies. Often, where there was kalcion there were hot springs. That was what got her father set on mining this particular area. Jenala's father built a room above the hot springs that ran through the bluff.

"I'm done," said Jenala, putting down her shovel. "I can't do anymore today and I'm not working tomorrow. We need to rest. Both of us have been working nonstop for two weeks."

"I couldn't agree more. Why don't you show me your valley tomorrow? Who knows we may get lucky and run into Zlaten. I'd be glad to get this all over with."

"Yes, then you wouldn't have to stay all winter."

"Oh, I intend to stay the winter. That was our agreement and whether or not I'm lucky enough to kill Zlaten before then, I intend to stay."

"Thank you. I can certainly use the help. And the company. Are you ready to check my seams?"

"Yes, let's go."

Jenala removed her shirt and started on the bandage. They'd changed it every third day and it was healing well. Santro cleaned her back and then rewrapped it every time.

"Put your arms out to your sides and let

me remove the bindings. You would think," he scolded, "after the number of times we have done this you would stop trying to unbind yourself. You know you can't do it."

"One of these times I'm going to be able to do it. I'm stubborn that way. I keep after something until I master it."

"Well, this you will not master, because you have been bound for the last time. Let me clean your back to make sure."

There was no dining room just a table and four chairs in the kitchen. She sat backwards in one of the kitchen chairs leaning forward with her arms wrapped around the back of the chair. Santro sat behind her and cleaned her wound. She was complaining of itching, a sure sign of healing.

Every time he'd cleaned her back,

Santro was torn between fury at Zlaten for his cowardly wounding of her and his own sexual excitement seeing and touching her breasts when he bound them.

He admired her. Her mother had died when she was just five. Raised by her father, she'd become like a son to him rather than a daughter. She fought like a man, worked in the mine like a man and had no modesty, like a man.

She drove him crazy…just like a woman.

"Would you like to join me in the steam room above the hot spring?"

"Yes." He'd thought it was a great idea until he saw her in there wrapped in only a short towel. He wore a robe and was now clutching the towel he'd brought in front of him, as his body responded to the sight of her. Damn! She didn't have a modest bone in her body and didn't have a clue how she affected him. Actually, she was wearing a towel. He thought that was a consideration on her part, until she dropped it before entering the pool.

"Come in. The water is wonderful." She flipped onto her back and floated in the steamy water. "Do you have any idea how awful it is not to be able to bathe for two weeks? I *was* starting to smell like Lottie." She laughed heartily at her jest.

Santro managed not to gawk. She stayed on her back. All of her glorious body displayed, not for his pleasure, but for her comfort.

He tried to remember she was his partner, he'd seen her topless on numerous occasions when he changed her bandages.

This wasn't much different. Ha! Who was he trying to fool? It was totally different. There was nothing medicinal about his thoughts now. He wasn't doctoring her, trying to cause her as little pain as possible.

Mesmerized, he watched her play. Swimming backwards, diving under and coming up on the far side of the pool, her glorious red hair a shimmering cloak about her.

"Santro. Santro are you listening to me? Come in the water. It will ease your muscles and make you feel better."

He carefully weighed his options and turned around to leave the room. She was too much temptation for the best of men and at that point in time, he was definitely not the best of men.

"Where are you going?"

"I, uh, remembered something I must do before our foray tonight." He wasn't lying. He had to get his wayward body under control.

"Oh, all right. I'll be out shortly. Lottie will be ready for her tequati and will be heading for the river."

That night they carried out their reconnaissance mission. They followed Lottie down to the river as she made her nightly journey to forage for food.

They found Zlaten's camp easily. If he'd been trying to hide it, he failed miserably. There were two men at camp. Zlaten was not one of them. Santro assumed he was doing his own recon of their house. They would know soon enough if he tried to breech the house defenses.

"He's not here," whispered Jenala.

"I know. He must be at the house doing the same thing that we are. We'll know soon if he tries to break in to the house, we'll be able to hear the alarm down here. And," Santro chuckled, "without the proper ear protection, Zlaten and any of his men that are with him, will be deaf for the next two days."

No sooner had he said it than a piercing whistle echoed throughout the valley. "Time for us to leave. Here, put these in your ears until we get home and can turn the alarm off." He handed her a set of ear plugs from out of his pocket.

Home. He really did think of it as home. After only two weeks, the dome house had become home or was it Jenala who made it feel like home. He wasn't supposed to fall for his partner, he kept telling himself that.

But he was, fast. It started when he first had her in his arms back in Rucem. Carrying her to the nupenian and again at breakfast the next morning. Every time he touched her the recognition was there. The electricity. Every time he fell deeper under her spell.

He felt things he'd never allowed himself before. He wanted a home and all that came with it. Children and most of all, a wife. Jenala as a wife, his wife. Had she been a member of his tribe he would have claimed her during the claiming ceremony. But she wasn't. She was free to participate in the ceremony if she wanted, or to remain free. Suddenly, he needed to know. Would she participate in the rite of claiming? Would she consider his claiming of her or was marriage the only option? Or perhaps neither, perhaps she wanted no liaisons with anyone.

Unfortunately for him, they needed to remain quiet on the trek back to the house. After they got back and assured themselves that all was well, he would broach the subject.

All was not well. When they returned to the house, they saw the dome had blaster marks on it. It had not been breached but was damaged and weakened. Lottie's barn had not fared as well. The blasters had taken out some of the supports and the roof had collapsed inward. They ran inside the house and Santro shut off the alarm. He touched her arm then took out his ear plugs. Jenala followed suit.

"They covered their tracks well. Do you suppose they were searching for the mine entrance or for us?" asked Jenala.

"My guess would be for the mine entrance. As dishonorable as Zlaten is, I don't believe he would try to use a blaster to kill us. Seeing as blasters are illegal here, I'm surprised he would have one. Though I don't suppose I should be. We both have kalcion swords made by the Nerutas. He has seen both of us in action and knows that blasters would be useless against us given our skill."

"True. Too bad Lottie wasn't home. She would have protected her barn from them. I guess our work tomorrow will be to repair or rebuild the barn," she said. "I'll have to assess it in the daylight. Perhaps it's not as bad as it looks in the dark."

It was worse. Only three of the support beams for the roof were intact. Two in the front and one in the back of the building kept the roof from total collapse. They would have to try and salvage what they could, but if they were to repair it completely, they would have to go to town and get more wood.

"That was his plan. He'd get us away from the house and he can search it at his leisure. No quick raids in the dark, but a thorough, systematic search for the mine. How long has he been in the valley?"

"My father was killed six months ago. He's been camping in the valley almost ever since. I keep wondering what he's waiting for. He stays away because of Lottie, but in town, he caught me by surprise in that alley. Caught me without Lottie."

Santro thought about it for a moment. "He's been searching the valley for the mine. It never occurred to him until he could find it nowhere else that the mine entrance might be in one of the buildings on this bluff. Obviously, he started with Lottie's barn and then tried the house. Might have made it in, had it not been for the alarm he triggered."

"But he didn't. Thank you for that."

"That's what I'm here for. To help you in any way I can."

"I thought you only wanted to kill Zlaten."

He looked at her hard. "My priorities have changed."

"Oh." She looked at her feet. "I see."

"No, I don't think you do. I want you Jenala," he closed the gap between them. "I know that my appearance is not repugnant to you. I would claim you if that is your preference."

"You would." Jenala didn't know whether to be flattered or pissed off. "Just so you can have sex with me?"

"Yes. No. It is not only to have sex with you. I have never wanted anyone the way I want you."

"Santro. I am not for claiming. I will marry, as my parents did or nothing. There is no claiming. We have a long winter ahead. If this is a problem for you, then perhaps you should leave now."

Santro backed up a step. "I am not leaving. I accept your proposal."

"You what? You accept my…my what?"

"Your proposal of marriage. I accept."

"You're crazy. I didn't propose."

"Ah, but you did. You said you will marry or nothing. Since I'm not leaving and you won't be claimed, marrying is the only solution which you proposed. Therefore, we will marry."

"No, we won't."

"Jenala," he said, taking her hands in his. "We would be very good together. We have common interests and goals. You know that I'm not marrying you for your mine, I'm a very wealthy man. You don't find my scar or lack of eye off putting and I find your use of a sword very attractive indeed. Actually, I admire you very much."

She was taken aback. He wanted her, not her mine. He admired her. Didn't think her odd for taking on a man's work or learning a man's skill. And she was very attracted to him, but marry him?

"I'm flattered but—" she tried to pull her hands away from his. She couldn't think straight, when he was touching her like this. She hadn't felt this way when he changed her bandages. Was that because all she could feel then was pain? But now, there were no bandages, the pain was gone and he was touching her. His thumb worried small circles into her palm. Around and around. Her breath rose and fell with each tiny revolution. There was a stirring in her core. Attraction. Sexual attraction. It ran through her like fire from the little circles on her palms to the moisture she now felt between her legs. Krios!

"Don't say no yet. As you said, we have all winter." He raised his hand to her cheek and gently caressed it.

"I can't…" she resisted.

"You can," he moved in closer, his breath, sweet and clean on her lips.

"But,"

"No buts," his lips met hers, quashing any arguments she had.

All thought flew from her mind and the only thing she wanted was to get closer. She wrapped her arms around his neck, then he broke the kiss.

"My sweet, Jenala. You tempt me woman. You will say, yes, eventually. I can wait." He walked to his room and shut the door behind him.

CHAPTER 4

Days turned into weeks but Zlaten didn't try to break in again. They repaired the barn, reusing as much of the wood as possible. They were able to replace most of the walls and three quarters of the roof, but part of it was still open to the sky and the elements. Lottie had lots of fur and would be fine, but Jenala didn't like it nonetheless.

They took turns at lookout and guard duties for the first week after the attempted break in. After that, since there were no immediate threats, they relied on the alarm system. She wondered if Zlaten was still feeling the effects of his first attack and that was why he hadn't tried again.

Santro made no attempts to kiss her and they didn't talk about marriage. Jenala was beginning to think she'd imagined the whole thing. Santro was kind, gentle and polite but that was all. In the last two weeks he hadn't even hinted that he wanted more than friendship.

It frustrated the hell out of her. His kiss awakened something deep inside her. Desire. She'd never felt it before. But, she did with him. She wanted to explore these feelings but how was she to do that without agreeing to marriage?

Just like all things in her life, she faced this head on. That morning over their meal she asked him. "Why haven't you tried to kiss me again?"

"I thought you didn't want my attentions."

"That was before." She suddenly wondered if this was such a good idea after all.

"Before what?"

"Before...you...kissed me. I liked it. I felt...something I've never felt before and I would like to explore it."

"The only way I can help you explore your new feelings is if you agree to our marriage.'

"You realize we would have to go to town to find a theologian? And we can't do that because the snow has closed the pass."

"I do. But if you agree to marry me, that is as binding to me as any words said by a stranger."

She thought about it before answering. "I suppose. I've never been known to break my word. What about you? Will you keep your word?"

"Yes, my lady, I keep my word. It is my bond. Just so there's complete understanding, I will say the words that bind me to you."

He turned to her, "Jenala Delasa, I take you to be my wedded wife. I will care for you and keep you safe for all the days I live."

"Santro Baltin, I…I…I'm scared. I've never contemplated anything like this. You make me feel so different."

He stepped forward and took her hands in his. "I can help ease you and help you explore these new feelings you have. I'm quite pleased you are having them. They show your interest in exploring your body and letting me explore it with you."

His thumbs made those lazy circles on her palm. She couldn't concentrate on anything but those circles. And she ached deep inside. Her arms were weak and tingles traveled up and down her spine. All from some little circles.

She took a deep breath. "Santro Baltin, I take you for my husband. I will endeavor to make you happy and will also protect you with my life."

He closed the gap between, took her face in his hands and lowered his lips to hers. The kiss was gentle, sweet. She tried to pull back, but his lips followed hers. His tongue darted out and tickled the seam of her lips. She smiled and opened a little. That was all the invitation he needed. His tongue plunged inside and began its duet with hers. Gentle, touching, retreating, touching.

It was making her crazy. She grabbed his head and held it while she kissed him. Her tongue entered his mouth and dueled with his. The kiss deepened. There was only him, only this moment, this kiss.

He pulled away, breathing hard. "Jenala, you are going to kill me with your kisses."

She stiffened. "I'm sorry if they are not to your liking."

"On the contrary. Your kisses are very much to my liking. There are other things we can explore together." To prove his point he pulled her close and rubbed his throbbing erection against her. "Many more things."

"Oh." Understanding dawned on her.

"Should we go to your bedroom?"

"The bed is bigger in your room."

"I don't want the first time we make love to be on my father's bed."

"I understand." He picked her up in his arms as though she weighed no more than feathers and carried her to his room. He let her slide down his body and she felt his erection. When it reached the apex of her legs, he stopped her progress and held her there. Against him. Let her feel his need for her.

"Do you feel how much I want you?" He moved a little and the tip of his cock rubbed the lips above her nub, sending little shock waves through her.

"I feel it. Teach me more."

"I intend to, my sweet. We will explore each other. Anything you want, nothing is off limits.  You may ask and explore my body as I will yours.  You are my wife and I am your husband."

"Yes.  It sounds wonderful.  Where do we start?"

"We start by getting out of these clothes."

He set her on her feet and turned his back to get shed of his clothes.  When he turned back Jenala was naked, standing there more than a little embarrassed.

"I don't understand it.  You've seen me naked.  Swimming and when you changed my bandages.  I wasn't embarrassed then.  But now, when we're going to make love, I am.

"Before, when you were swimming you were confident, you were in control.  With the bandages, it was medical not sexual.

This time it is entirely sexual. I intend to explore every inch of your delicious, delectable body."

"Delicious. Delectable. It sounds like you mean to eat me."

"Oh, I do, among other things." With those words he kissed her and backed her toward the bed, fell with her onto it, bracing himself on his arms so as not to crush her with the weight of his big body. Yet, he never broke the kiss until he rolled to his side and leaned up on one elbow.

He rubbed her belly. Moved up to her breasts. He gently squeezed them, rolled a nipple between his thumb and forefinger, first one and then the other.

Fire burned through her body, turning to liquid at her core.

Santro rained kisses over her breasts

took a nipple into his mouth and sucked. Hard. His tongue darted forward to joust with her nipple.

He moved until he was positioned between her legs exposing her completely to him. He kissed and laved her heated skin with his tongue. He moved ever downward toward his goal. What parts he missed with his tongue, his hand soothed, caressing every inch of her he could reach.

He parted the curls hiding her love bud from him, then took his tongue and started circling her clitoris with the hard, pointed tip of his tongue. Darting in and out, back and forth across the sensitized nub.

She squeezed and played with her own breasts. The sensation of Santro's tongue on her intensified when she squeezed her nipples. She felt it down to her core. His mouth played with her, sending waves of pleasure through her.

He took one finger then two and put them into her vagina and stretched them apart, preparing her for his entry. She may not have done this before but she wasn't ignorant of the workings of her own body. She'd seen his shaft, standing tall and proud, she was sure he wouldn't fit.

His mouth stayed on her, as much as was possible while he stretched her, sucking and teasing until she thought she would die with anticipation and need. She searched for something, some pinnacle, just out of her reach.

She held his head down, trying to get him closer. Reaching. Reaching. He sucked hard. His tongue flicked faster until she shattered. Her world suddenly expanded to include all the stars in the universe. "Oh my God. Santro!"

He continued to lave her with his tongue, slower and slower, till she quieted. Then he rose over her, placed his cock at the entrance to her vagina and entered slowly, teasingly. He kissed her and whispered against her lips, "I'm sorry for any pain I'm about to cause you."

He pulled almost all the way out of her then thrust hard and fast as far as he could, until he was buried to the hilt. Jenala felt a small amount of pain but he let her get used to him as long as he could before he moved in her again.

"You feel so good, so tight." He thrust into her again and again. She got down the rhythm and pulled back when he did then forward with him, burying him deeper with each thrust.

He reached between them and rubbed her clit again. She didn't think it was possible for her to climax again but she did and he followed her crying out her name.

Cuddling up to him she said, "That was spectacular!"

He laughed. "That, my sweet, was an introduction to love making. It will get better and better between us. I promise."

They fell into sleep. The sleep of those sated by unbridled passion and satisfying sex. The sleep of lovers.

Before sunrise the next morning they were awakened by alarms going off in Lottie's barn and Lottie hooting and neighing. They could almost feel her stomps.

Jenala grabbed her sword and was up in

a flash, only to find Santro had beat her and was dressing.

"We have to be careful. This could be a ruse to get us out of the house and ambush us."

"How is it that you know what he might be thinking?" She asked, pulling on her boots.

"Because I will never underestimate him again. It's what I would do if I was in his place."

Jenala dressed and looked at Santro. "Come with me. I have an escape tunnel out of the house which I have not showed you yet. Father always thought that thieves were a possibility since the mine was famous in stories."

"You didn't trust me," he teased.

"I didn't know you. But now I must

show you everything."

They entered the mine and took the left shaft. It wasn't well lit as the other shafts and now he knew why. It wasn't a mine tunnel but an escape tunnel.

"I never thought I'd actually have to use this, but Father insisted we put it in. It will take us above the mine to the top of the bluff. We'll be able to see exactly what they are doing without being seen ourselves."

"Lead on. This is ingenious. Your father designed this very well."

"Thank you. I thought and still believe he was an amazing man."

"There is no doubt in my mind. He would have to be special, just to take on the raising of you, without a woman."

She looked at him and saw the twinkle in his eyes. "You're teasing me. I can tell."

"How would you know that?"

"When you've been married as long as I have, you just know these things about your husband."

His bark of laughter echoed in the tunnel. "I like your sense of humor."

They wound their way through and up the mountain. Santro noticed several cracks of kalcion, very small, but full of kalcion none-the-less. At the top was a door. It slid open and he saw that it looked like just another boulder from the outside.

They walked forward about twenty feet and looked down at the dome and the entire valley beyond. They saw Zlaten and his men had the dome surrounded and Lottie was locked in her barn.

"If we go down this side, we can unleash Lottie. We'll have to be careful not to draw their attention," whispered Jenala.

As quietly as possible, they worked their way down through the trees and brushy undergrowth, to Lottie's barn. Jenala went to the back barn door and opened it. Zlaten and his gang were on the other side of the barn and wouldn't know what hit them. A pissed off snarlot was a thing to behold. And fear.

Jenala soothed Lottie long enough for Santro to open the front barn door. Lottie immediately charged out of the barn and directly at Zlaten. He screamed, pushed one of his compatriots in front of him and took off down the mountain, screaming like a twelve year old girl. Lottie stomped the man Zlaten had pushed, crushing his head under her hooves. Two of the other men tried to come to their friend's aid and were ripped apart by Lottie's toothy beak. The last two tried to run past Santro and Jenala, but were met with swords. It was obvious these men were not well trained in the use of a sword. Santro and Jenala both severely wounded their opponents before letting them go back to Zlaten. "Tell Zlaten not to come back. There will be dire consequences for him and anyone he brings with him," shouted Jenala to the retreating forms of the two men.

Lottie came over to Jenala and nudged her with her beak. "Sweet girl, you did good, yes you did," Jenala cooed while scratching Lottie behind the ears.

"I think this girl deserves a big treat, how about you?" asked Santro.

" I agree. Can you go get the raw emul from the cold keeper? We were going to have it for dinner, but I think Lottie deserves it more."

"Agreed. She performed very well," said Santro. He went over to them and petted Lottie's neck. She nudged him just like she had Jenala. He took the hint and scratched her ears, too.

Never in his life did he imagine he'd be scratching the ears of a snarlot. Yet when Lottie started purring, Santro felt a contentment he'd not had before. This was unconditional love and acceptance, all shown in one sound—purring.

He wanted to make Jenala purr. He wanted the unconditional acceptance that she gave him. But he wanted love, too. She wasn't repelled by his scar, as proven by her marrying him--without a theologian, no less. He knew as did she that the marriage would not stand up legally, but for him it was binding. As far as he was concerned Jenala was his wife, forever. Now all he had to do was figure out how to get his wife to fall in love with him.

*****

Zlaten watched from a safe distance as his men were stomped and torn limb from limb by the snarlot. The beast was supposed to be locked up. How did Santro and the bitch escape from the house without being seen? There had to be another way into the house and he had to find it. Maybe it would also prove to be the entrance to the mine. The mine that would be his, should have been his by now.

He'd spent all of his beras in the last six months, searching for the mine. He had to have *this* mine. The Delasa mine was legend. It was rumored to have the richest vein of kalcion ever found. Oliria Delasa found the mine ten years ago. He had to have found the vein by now. Must have.

If the silly old man had just given him the location of the mine he could have been rich by now. Instead he was broke, three of his men were dead and he was no closer to his goal.

Damn Oliria Delasa and his demon seed daughter.

*****

It was easy enough to feed Jenala's lust; he could have sex with her all day and night. Love, though, that was something totally different and out of his realm of knowledge. He'd never found anyone before he wanted to love him or anyone he thought he could love. Jenala was that person. He respected her and admired her. Perhaps that was part of love. Who knew?

The first thing he must do is show her is the kalcion cracks in the escape tunnel. They looked like the kind of cracks he found in his mine just before he hit the big payout vein. She would know then he was truly her partner and not there to take advantage of her. Especially, now that they were having sex.

He was also kind and gentle and protective of her. Tonight she would probably be too sore to make sweet, slow love to her but tomorrow she should be recovered sufficiently.

Tonight he would just hold her or give her oral sex. Perhaps they could explore each other's bodies. Just touching, feeling, discovering.

It was still early, when they finished burying the bodies. They went inside to have breakfast. Santro had gotten coffee from his friend Sunev. She made emul rehydrated in a sauce made from tingo root and fried up some fresh tequati that Lottie had put on the doorstep this morning. The coffee was from a place called Earth. Sunev had gotten it in trade. Jenala liked the coffee but still preferred hot aeta.

"I have something to show you," Santro said rising from the table. "I saw some cracks of kalcion when we were in the escape tunnel and I think we should concentrate our efforts there."

"There are cracks all over the mine. What's special about these?"

"They're the same type of crack I found leading to the main vein in my own mine.

These cracks are single lines, with no branches coming off of them."

"Okay. It sounds promising and it can't be any worse than what we've been digging."

They went to work in the escape tunnel. After a full day's labor, Jenala had enough kalcion to by the new coat she needed, but that was more than they'd gotten before.

"We didn't do as well as I'd hoped," she said wistfully. "I don't know why I thought we'd hit the mother lode so quickly."

"I, too, had high hopes but we must be patient. Tomorrow we'll start again."

He dropped his tools and walked over to her. "Tonight, however, we have another lesson in lovemaking."

"I look forward to it, *after* we have bathed. I have some questions about lovemaking," she leaned back in his arms, trusting he would not drop her. "Can I put my mouth on you, as you did on me?"

He almost dropped her! He was startled and inordinately pleased. She wanted to make love to him with her mouth. "Yes, you can. I'd be a very happy man should you desire to do so."

She grinned up at him. "I do, but not till after we have both bathed and taken a swim in the hot springs. We are filthy as allorats and are starting to smell like them, too."

Santro laughed. "That we are. Let's go."

He wanted her more powerfully than he'd ever wanted a woman. He'd had women throwing themselves at him since he was a green boy, but he'd never wanted one like he did Jenala. That's the real reason he'd wanted to marry her. She wouldn't have him any other way and he wouldn't force himself on her but he'd *had* to have her, to brand her, to make her his and his alone.

This time when Santro entered the steam room, he did not hide himself but let his towel drop and let her look at him. Fully aroused and ready for her. And look she did. Her tongue darted out to wet her dry lips. He nearly came then and there. Lucky for him he had supreme self-control.

Santro was wonderful to look at from his dark auburn hair and incredible chest to his impressive cock standing at attention. He was every girls dream or at least this girls dream. And he was her husband to boot. How lucky could she get? If she could have all that and his love, then it would be perfect.

She was no fool. She knew their 'marriage' would never stand the scrutiny of the law but she didn't care. Santro would keep his word. It was his law and his honor. And she would keep hers. She had no desire for another man. She'd *never* had a desire for anyone before him.

Wanting Santro blindsided her. It was totally unexpected and unplanned. Perhaps it was because he saved her life or because of their close proximity to each other, whatever the reason she wanted to be with him more every day.

Now here she was sitting in a hot spring looking at him with his fully erect cock and she wanted only to take him into her. Into her mouth, into her vagina. Any way she could get him to be part of her.

"If I didn't already know that we fit together, I'd have thought you too big for me."

"Ah," he chuckled. "That explains the fascination."

"Come in the water. It's nice. I want to feel you next to me. Actually, I want more than that but first let's have the warm water relax our muscles…before we exert them again."

She hung on to the sides of the pool, while her body floated up, giving him what she hoped was a tantalizing offering.

No sooner had she uttered the invitation than he dove into the water. The next thing she knew he had her legs and was pulling them down and wrapping them around his waist. She was fully open to him.

"Can you feel me, my sweet? Feel how

much I want you. Even the hot water doesn't diminish my desire for you. My need for your warmth not that of the water."

He thrust into her, strong and powerful. She gasped with surprise and delight. Unexpected or not she was ready for him. Always. Just thinking about him made her hot and wet. She almost came just picturing him fully aroused, coming into her as he was now.

She met him thrust for thrust. Jenala leaned back and braced herself on the side of the pool or she would have floated away.

He kissed her, this tongue mingling with hers. In and out to the rhythm of his thrusts. He kissed and tongued her neck, his whiskers made her shiver with pleasure. For just a moment he sucked the side of her neck, surely leaving a love bite, marking her for all the world to see, as his wife.

He lifted her legs, one over each arm and carried her from the pool. He stayed in her and with each step gave her a gentle shot to her body as her clitoris rubbed up and down against his base of his cock.

They fell together onto her bed. He began driving into her in earnest, hard, in and out. He suckled her breasts, intensifying the pleasant sensations, settling at the very core where her body met his.

He reached between them and rubbed her clit. She moaned with pleasure as each movement of his finger brought her closer. She held him close to her breast. "Suck. Suck hard. Take all my nipple into your mouth and suck me."

He did and she came. Shaking with her release, wave after wave of pleasure washed over her. She swore the stars overhead shone brighter, as though they too shared her climax.

His eye was heavy lidded. He thrust harder and harder, then one pump and he was buried to the very tip of her womb. He shouted and pumped into her again and again as his climax overtook him. He collapsed on her and she welcomed his weight. She was closest to him, not just in body, but in mind, after their lovemaking. It was as though they both let go and their bodies were completely honest with each other.

No pretense, just raw passion.

## CHAPTER 5

He watched every day. Watched and waited. Zlaten couldn't wait any longer. He was out of beras and his men were grumbling about the danger and their lack of payment. There were only three of them now and two were still injured from the attack by the snarlot. No it had to be now or it would never be.

He'd been watching. Every day now, they were starting to dismantle the barn. That in itself was odd, since they'd taken great care to rebuild it as much as possible for the vicious beast the bitch called a pet. Now they were tearing it down, board by board and taking the boards into the house.

It finally hit him. He'd been looking in the wrong place for the entrance to the mine. All this time. Lost. The entrance was in the house. The crafty old man had hidden it from the world. In plain sight.

Santro and Jenala never left together. One would stay in the house while the other got the wood. They must be working the mine and they must have found the mother lode, otherwise they wouldn't be taking apart her beloved snarlot's home. There had to be another way in. Oliria was too smart to make only one entrance and he remembered that they had just appeared the last time he'd attacked the house. But he'd been looking for it for six months to no avail.

He needed to take action. Santro and Jenala always left the house separately. They'd gotten complacent since he hadn't done anything for the past three weeks. He'd let his men heal and he watched. Always watching. He knew their routine now. The next time Santro went to the barn for wood, he would enter the house. He could take Jenala, especially in close quarters and if he was really lucky, she'd be in the mine and he'd kill two salies with one stone.

*****

They'd found it. The mother lode. Jenala had never seen so much kalcion in her life. The cracks that Santro found in the escape tunnel led to the biggest vein either of them had ever seen. It was two feet across and who knew how deep. They chipped away at it. Filled buckets and bags. This large amount couldn't be handled by the exchange in Rucem. It would have to go to the next kalcion market at Sepiwa.

Lottie was going to have a ball scaring the new people at the kalcion market. By that time, there would be a new little Baltin. What would Santro say when she told him? Would he be happy?

The market was seven months away. Jenala couldn't help but wonder what would happen when Santro captured or killed Zlaten. Either way he would have to take him back to the Otula tribe. He would again be their champion and able to challenge to be the next Valmud. It was an honor, something he'd worked for. Been trained for all his life. She couldn't blame him if he chose that life. The problem was it wasn't what she chose for her life. Her life was here in the valley. The life she chose for her child was here. But she would not force Santro to accept this life. He was born for greater things.

It didn't matter how much kalcion came out of the mine. Her home was and always would be the valley and the house under the dome.

From behind her she heard the hiss of a sword being slid from it's scabbard. She turned shovel in hand and blocked the first blow, then a second and third. The shovel was unwieldy and she was tiring quickly.

"You couldn't face me like a man, Zlaten. You had to sneak up behind me like a coward? Is that what you did to my father? Did he trust you or did you catch him unaware when his back was turned. Did you lie in wait for him like the zogamac you are?"

"Insults will only get you killed sooner, bitch. You should have sold to me. The Delasa Mine belongs to me. I want it. I offered to buy it. But your father laughed at me. It was the last time he laughed at anyone. He was a stupid man. You never turn your back on your enemy."

He struck another blow, this one breaking the shovel handle. Jenala dropped the shovel's scoop and used the handle as a sword and blocked the next blow.

"Zlaten!" Santro appeared behind him in the tunnel. "You can't fight me like a man, so you attack my wife. Turn and defend yourself or I will run you through where you stand."

Zlaten turned. Attacked. Their swords clashed again and again. Jenala stood transfixed. She watch Santro play with him, watched as Zlaten tired quickly his strokes slower and less powerful.

"Jenala move!" Santro yelled at her as Zlaten turned and slashed his sword downward. She dropped and rolled, his sword missing everything except her arm, giving her another wound, though not a serious one.

Santro jabbed his sword, hitting Zlaten through the right side. Zlaten dropped his sword and fell to his knees. "No. This can't be happening. I never lose."

"You're wrong. You always lose. Every time you fight less than honorably you lose."

"You've killed me." He took his bloody hand away from his side.

"If only I had. Unfortunately, you'll live. We'll take you to the nupenian in Rucem. He'll use his wand on you and you'll be like new when you stand trial for the murders of Kreston Baltin and Oliria Delasa. I wonder how many others there are that we'll never know about. How many more innocent people have you murdered?"

Santro turned to Jenala. "I have to take him in for justice to be served. I know I said I'd kill him but I can't in good conscience. He is unarmed now. I'm not a murderer."

"I understand. It is the honorable choice. But," she clutched her shoulder, "right now I need you to bandage my shoulder." She removed her hand and blood seeped from the wound.

He took off his shirt. "Take this and hold it tight against the wound to stem the bleeding. I'll get the liquid bandage." He nodded toward Zlaten who lay passed out on the floor. "Watch." Santro poured water on Zlaten's head. He sputtered awake.

He shook his head and sprayed water everywhere. "Killing me isn't enough, now you're going to torture me too?"

"If only I could."

After caring for Jenala, Santro moved over to Zlaten. He closed his wound with the liquid, just enough to stem the bleeding. Then he bandaged and wrapped the wound. Zlaten would stay alive to meet his punishment from the council and the local authorities in Rucem.

Now Zlaten had to go meet Lottie. She would have to carry them to Rucem. It did not go well. Lottie stomped and snorted, nipped at him with her beak but in the end, she allowed him to ride her with Santro along.

"I'm not going with you." Jenala said.

"Why?"

"Someone needs to stay here to protect the mine. Zlaten may still have men out there and--"

"All the more reason for you to come with me," argued Santro.

She put her arms around his neck and leaned back, looking up into his beloved face. "I must stay. You know it. I won't leave my valley to marauders and thieves."

"That's right," sneered Zlaten. "My

men will get you. Just wait and see."

Santro's fist shot out and landed square in the middle of Zlaten's face breaking his nose.

He turned back to Jenala. "How can I leave you here alone?"

"I'll be fine. You forget I've been alone before. Even when father was alive I was alone often for months at a time."

"I know. But that doesn't mean I have to like it." He bent his head and kissed her.

"Oh, pweeze. Can we go, 'fore I bweed to deaf." Zlaten said, his head tilted back to stop his nose bleed.

"If you don't shut up, I'll hit you again."

Zlaten backed away. "All wight. All wight. Don't hit me again."

"Now that he knows he's not going to die, he's going to be a pain in the ass all the way back to Rucem. I'll send Lottie home when I get there. She should be back here by tomorrow morning. In the mean time, stay inside, keep the alarms on and the entrances all locked. Okay?" He leaned down and kissed her again heedless of Zlaten and his protests. "Promise me."

"I promise. Until Lottie gets home, then she will protect me as she always has."

She saw a shadow cross his face. Uncertainty. She strove to remove it. "I'll be fine. I promise to be especially cautious." She wanted to ask him if he would return, but was afraid she wouldn't like the answer. Afraid he would choose the Valmud over her. She couldn't face that, not now, not with her secret.

*****

It had been six months.  She'd heard a few times from Santro.  Letters he'd sent to Brenton and he'd forwarded to Jenala.  He'd gotten Zlaten to Brenton, who'd sent him to the new town doctor.  A young woman named Riza Lamrona.  Zlaten was tried and found guilty for the murder of Jenala's father Oliria and then was extradited to the Otula.  Once there, Zlaten was again tried for murder and found guilty.  The council sentenced him to life on the prison planet Solara.

She knew after the trial Santro would be champion of the Otula again.  It would be his place to challenge for the Valmud.  He would win, she had no doubt.

Jenala rubbed her still expanding tummy.  The baby, her baby, kicked as though to tell her to 'leave me alone'.

Jenala laughed and rubbed her belly again.

"What makes you laugh, wife?" Santro stood in the doorway, his large body casting a shadow over her.

Jenala turned and faced him. The result of their lovemaking evident for him to see.

"A baby? You're having a baby? Why didn't you tell me? Why…?"

Jenala turned away, tears too close to the surface for her to look upon his beloved face. "I didn't want this to sway you. I wanted you to come back of your own free will. Because you wanted to, because you…"

He was by her side in two long strides. "Jenala. Look at me, love." He raised her face to him. "I came as soon as I was able. It took much longer than I expected to find someone to replace me as Valmud. My father no longer wants the position. He was ready to retire and have me succeed him. I explained that I could not do that. But I couldn't leave until I'd made arrangements for my tribe to go on without me."

"I never wanted to be a burden to you. Neither of us." She patted her belly.

Santro held her face gently in his palms and wiped away her tears with his thumbs. "You are my wife, Jenala Delasa Baltin and I love you more than life itself."

"You do?"

"I've been yours since I saw your glorious red hair flying about as you fought with Zlaten. Then when you looked up at me, with so much trust in those beautiful blue eyes of yours, I fell completely, hopelessly in love with you."

"And I you. Since the moment I first saw you. I knew you would not harm me, that you would protect me. It was as though I'd met my other half, my soul, my heart."

"And what of our little one?" He touched her stomach with such gentleness, Jenala almost cried. "When is he or she due?"

"In less than a month. I have already thought of a name for a boy. Kreston Oliria Baltin, to honor both of our fallen family. Do you like it?"

"Very much." He took her in his arms, her back to his chest, and rested his arms across her belly. "What if it is a girl?"

"I have not given it much thought. What would you like?"

"I'd like to name her after our mothers. My mother's name was Jenuvia," said Santro. "What was your mothers name?"

"Vian. How about Jenuvia Vian Baltin if it is a girl, which I'm certain it is not."

"How can you be so sure?"

"This little one has been fighting with me since I was able to feel him. He is just to ornery to be a girl."

Santro laughed. "So girls are not capable of being tiny terrorists? I would bet your father would have disagreed."

Jenala pouted. "I'll have you know I was the most well behaved child." Then with a naughty laugh, "most of the time."

He hugged her close. "I don't care what variety of child it is. He or she is wanted and loved by both of us. We will raise them right here in this valley, safe and secure. Of course, we'll have to work on having many more children. They'll need to have each other to play with and…" he paused.

"And what?"

"Mommy and Daddy need to perfect their baby making skills. And you know," he kissed her, "practice makes perfect."

*****

Santro and Jenala went to stay in town a full week before the baby was due. There was no way Santro was taking a chance with Jenala. He wanted the new doctor to deliver his child and make sure his wife was well taken care of.

Little Kreston Oliria Baltin did not arrive on time but was fifteen days late. He had his mother's fiery hair and his fathers green eyes. Luckily for his mother, he also had his father's gentle nature.